Cinderella

Retold by Heather Amery

Illustrated by Stephen Cartwright

Language consultant: Betty Root

Series editor: Jenny Tyler

There's a little yellow duck to find on every page.

That's Cinderella looking out of the window.

She lives with her nasty Stepmother and two ugly Stepsisters.
They are always really horrid to her.

They make her work all day.

She cleans the house and cooks the meals. She wears old clothes and sleeps in a cold, creepy room.

They are all asked to a Grand Ball at the palace.

The two Stepsisters are so excited. "We must have new dresses, and look our very best," they scream.

The great day comes.

The Stepsisters get ready for the Grand Ball. "May
I come?" asks Cinderella. "NO, NO, NO," they shout.

Cinderella sits down and cries.

Suddenly she sees her Fairy Godmother. "Do as I tell you and you shall go to the Ball," says Fairy Godmother.

"Bring me these things."

Cinderella brings Fairy Godmother a pumpkin, six white mice, a brown rat in a cage, and six green lizards.

Fairy Godmother waves her magic wand.

In a flash, the pumpkin is a coach, the mice are horses,
the rat a coachman and the lizards are footmen.

Then Cinderella has a lovely dress and shoes.

"Go to the Ball," says Fairy Godmother. "But you
must leave before the clock strikes midnight."

Cinderella goes to the palace.

The Prince meets her at the door. Everyone thinks she's a Princess. She has a lovely evening dancing with the Prince.

Then the clock strikes twelve.

"It's midnight. I must go," cries Cinderella. She runs down the palace stairs so fast one of her shoes falls off.

She runs all the way home.

She sits in the kitchen in her old clothes. Then the Stepsisters come home. They tell Cinderella about the Princess.

Next day, the Prince is very unhappy.

He wants to find the Princess. He has found her shoe.

"I'll marry the girl who can wear this shoe," he says.

The Stepsisters try on the shoe.

They push and pull. They scream and cry. The shoe is much too small for their big, ugly feet.

"May I try?" says Cinderella.

Of course, the shoe fits perfectly. Suddenly Fairy Godmother
appears and changes her clothes into a lovely dress.

"I have found you," says the Prince.

"Will you marry me?" "Yes, please." Cinderella says.

They live in the palace, and are always very happy.

This edition first published in 2003 by Usborne Publishing Ltd, 83-85 Saffron Hill, London EC1N 8RT, England. www.usborne.com
Copyright © 2003, 1996 Usborne Publishing Ltd.